TO THE EXTREME

Ice Climbing

by Angie Peterson Kaelberer

Reading Consultant:
Barbara J. Fox
Reading Specialist
North Carolina State University

Capstone
press

Mankato, Minnesota

Blazers is published by Capstone Press,
151 Good Counsel Drive, P.O. Box 669, Mankato, Minnesota 56002.
www.capstonepress.com

Library of Congress Cataloging-in-Publication Data
Kaelberer, Angie Peterson.
 Ice climbing / by Angie Peterson Kaelberer.
 p. cm.—(Blazers. To the extreme)
 Summary: "Describes the sport of ice climbing, including
equipment, techniques, and safety information"—Provided
by publisher.
 Includes bibliographical references and index.
 ISBN 0-7368-4398-1 (hardcover)
 ISBN 0-7368-6175-0 (softcover)
 1. Snow and ice climbing—Juvenile literature. I. Title. II. Series.
GV200.3.K34 2006
796.9—dc22   2005001433

Credits
Jason Knudson, set designer; Kate Opseth, book designer; Jo Miller,
 photo researcher; Scott Thoms, photo editor

Photo Credits
Art Directors, 21
Aurora/Scott Warren, 5, 6, 7, 8, 9
Bruce Coleman Inc./Mark Newman, cover
Corbis/Chris Rainier, 15; Don Mason, 25; Ken Redding, 28–29;
 Phil Schermeister, 22; Picimpact/Ashley Cooper, 12
Globe Photos, 13
Index Stock Imagery/Greg Epperson, 11, 16–17, 20, 27; Todd Powell, 19

The publisher does not endorse products whose logos may appear on objects in
images in this book.

**Capstone Press thanks John Harlin, editor, *American Alpine Journal*,
Hood River, Oregon, and his daughter, Siena, for their assistance with
this book.**

1 2 3 4 5 6 10 09 08 07 06 05

Table of Contents

Climbing a Frozen Waterfall

The climber grips the wall of ice.
Only his tools hold him 200 feet
(61 meters) above a frozen river.

The climber uses his climbing
tools to move into a better position.
Metal spikes attached to his boots
hold his feet in place.

The climber inches up the frozen waterfall. He moves slowly and carefully. The top is in sight!

Equipment

Ice climbers carry an ice axe and an ice hammer. They use the tools to stay balanced on the ice.

Ice axe

Ice hammer

Ice climbers wear crampons on their boots. The crampons have sharp, pointed spikes. They dig into ice walls.

Crampon

BLAZER FACT

Before they had crampons, climbers used ice axes to cut steps in the ice.

Climbers attach their ice tools to wrist leashes. The leashes support the weight of the climber with less strain on the hands.

BLAZER FACT

In the 1960s, Yvon Chouinard invented an ice axe with a curved pick. The axe made climbing steep ice easier.

Wrist leash

Ice Climber Diagram

Rope

Wrist leash

Helmet

Ice axe

Ice hammer

Ice screw

17

Climbing Methods

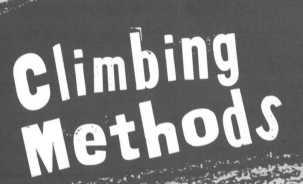

Ice climbers look for footholds. They try to keep their weight on their feet. Climbers rest their hands and arms this way.

Climbers front-point on steep
ice. They dig the front points of
their crampons deep into the ice.

Climbers use the monkey hang. This hold keeps arm muscles from becoming too tired.

BLAZER FACT

Ouray Ice Park opened in Colorado in 1995. It is the first park for ice climbers in the United States.

Safety

One climber belays while the other climbs. A rope connects the two climbers. The belayer holds the rope tight if the leader falls.

Leader

Rope

Belayer

Ice climbers dress for warmth. They wear layers of lightweight clothing. Helmets protect their heads from falling ice.

BLAZER FACT

Climbers wear gloves that resist both wind and water. They often carry more than one pair of gloves.

Scaling a tower
of ice!

Glossary

axe (AKS)—a tool with a sharp blade on the end of a handle

belay (bi-LAY)—to connect two climbers with a rope

crampon (KRAM-pahn)—a metal frame with pointed metal teeth that attaches to an ice climber's boots

foothold (FUT-hold)—a crack or chip in the ice where a climber can place a foot

front-point (FRUHNT-poynt)—to dig the front points of the crampons into the ice

wrist leash (RIST LEESH)—a strap with one end attached to a climber's wrist and the other end attached to an ice tool

Read More

George, Charles, and Linda George. *Ice Climbing*. Sports Alive! Mankato, Minn.: Capstone Press, 1999.

Oxlade, Chris. *Rock Climbing*. Extreme Sports. Minneapolis: Lerner, 2004.

Roberts, Jeremy. *Rock and Ice Climbing! Top the Tower*. Extreme Sports Collection. New York: Rosen, 2000.

Internet Sites

FactHound offers a safe, fun way to find Internet sites related to this book. All of the sites on FactHound have been researched by our staff.

Here's how:

1. Visit *www.facthound.com*
2. Type in this special code **0736843981** for age-appropriate sites. Or enter a search word related to this book for a more general search.
3. Click on the **Fetch It** button.

FactHound will fetch the best sites for you!

Index